D0723922

fenway
AND THE
BONE THIEVES

SNIFF OUT ALL THE

MAKE WAY FOR FENWAY!

CHAPTER BOOKS!

Fenway and the Bone Thieves

Fenway and the Frisbee Trick

DIG UP THESE MIDDLE GRADE BOOKS ABOUT FENWAY, TOO!

Fenway and Hattie

Fenway and Hattie and the Evil Bunny Gang

Fenway and Hattie Up to New Tricks

Fenway and Hattie in the Wild

fenway
AND THE
BONE THIEVES

VICTORIA J. COE

illustrated by
JOANNE LEW-VRIETHOFF

G. P. PUTNAM'S SONS

G. P. PUTNAM'S SONS
An imprint of Penguin Random House LLC, New York

First published in the United States of America by G. P. Putnam's Sons,
an imprint of Penguin Random House LLC, 2022

Text copyright © 2022 by Victoria J. Coe
Illustrations copyright © 2022 by Joanne Lew-Vriethoff

Penguin supports copyright. Copyright fuels creativity, encourages diverse
voices, promotes free speech, and creates a vibrant culture. Thank you for buy-
ing an authorized edition of this book and for complying with copyright laws
by not reproducing, scanning, or distributing any part of it in any form without
permission. You are supporting writers and allowing Penguin
to continue to publish books for every reader.

G. P. Putnam's Sons is a registered trademark of Penguin Random House LLC
Penguin Books & colophon are registered trademarks of Penguin Books Limited.

Visit us online at penguinrandomhouse.com

Library of Congress Cataloging-in-Publication Data is available.

Printed in the United States of America

ISBN 9780593406915 (hardcover)
1 3 5 7 9 10 8 6 4 2

ISBN 9780593406922 (paperback)
1 3 5 7 9 10 8 6 4 2

LSCC

Design by Marikka Tamura
Text set in Bodoni Six ITC Std

This book is a work of fiction. Any references to historical events, real people, or
real places are used fictitiously. Other names, characters, places,
and events are products of the author's imagination, and any resemblance to
actual events or places or persons, living or dead, is entirely coincidental.

The publisher does not have any control over and does not assume any
responsibility for author or third-party websites or their content.

To Tracey and Randi,
and for Marietta, who brought us
all together. —V.J.C.

To Max and Mattiece:
Life has been interesting, adventurous,
fun, and beautiful with you in it,
thank you. Love, Mama —J.L.V.

CONTENTS

1. THE TREAT PLACE . . . 1

2. THE PRIZE . . . 9

3. THE LADIES . . . 17

4. SQUIRREL TROUBLE! . . . 27

5. RAIN . . . 35

6. HOLES . . . 45

7. CHASE! . . . 55

8. THE DREAM . . . 63

9. SURPRISE . . . 71

10. THE BONE . . . 79

1

THE TREAT PLACE

Everyone knows that dogs are better than squirrels. Dogs make humans happy. Dogs live in houses. Dogs ride in cars. Squirrels do none of these things.

Squirrels go where they don't belong. Squirrels take things that aren't theirs. Squirrels are sneaky.

It's a good thing humans have dogs to keep them safe from squirrels.

Right now, I'm in the car with my family—Food Lady, Fetch Man, and Hattie—and no squirrels. I snuggle against Hattie in the back seat. She is the best short human ever.

She pats my head. "Good boy, Fenway," she coos. That's Human for "You're doing a great job." What can I say? I'm a professional.

I can hardly wait to find out where we're going.

The car pauses at the end of our street. I poke my head out the window. A sneaky squirrel is there on the sidewalk glaring up at me.

"Look at me, Rodent," I bark at him. "I'm riding in a car!"

He turns and scampers up a tree.

As the car speeds away, I add, "You'd better stay up there where you belong!"

There's nothing like a car ride. The breeze rushes through my fur. My nose sniffs oaks and pines and grass. My tail thumps against Hattie's leg. This is the life!

When the car turns, I smell another scent. It's the parking lot outside the Treat Place. That's the giant building with lots of dogs and humans—and toys and treats. Yippee!

I paw the door handle. "Hooray! Hooray!" I bark. "Let's get in there!"

Hattie giggles and opens the door. We hurry out of the car. I try to run straight into the Treat Place, but the leash holds me back. Of course Hattie wants me to wait for her. She loves going to the Treat Place as much as I do.

We lead Food Lady and Fetch Man inside. My tail swishes wildly. The Treat Place has rows and rows of awesome things to check out. And it smells great, like loads of other dogs. And have I mentioned the yummy treats? I'm going to show Hattie where to find them.

I stick my head into the first row. Wowee—toys! My tail wags faster.

"I could use a few more balls and squeakers and plushies," I bark to Hattie. But she doesn't give in. We follow Fetch Man and Food Lady to the next row.

I sniff there, too. Whoopee—treats! I smack my chops. "Let's get

some snacks," I whine. "I'm soooo hungry!"

"Fenway," Hattie says. She leads me away. "No."

My ears sag. Why aren't we getting any treats? What could be more important?

Food Lady steers a cart down another row, where Fetch Man grabs two big bags of kibble. And after that, we turn toward the back of the building. We are heading farther from the treats. I begin to get a bad feeling. This cannot be good.

2

THE PRIZE

We meet a friendly German Shepherd, but Hattie won't let us exchange bum sniffs. And then Fetch Man steers the cart down a row that smells like nasty cleaners. Yuck!

Food Lady stops and stares at the bottles on the shelves. She picks them up one by one. She studies

them as if they're actually interesting. Eventually, she puts one
in the cart and heads toward some
that smell even worse.

Ew! The odor reminds me of those horrible drops that Hattie rubs on the back of my neck. "No, Hattie," I plead as she follows Fetch Man and Food Lady. "Let's skip the yucky drops and go back to the treats."

But we don't. Food Lady tosses *two* boxes of yucky drops into the cart. Just when I think this trip cannot get any more terrible, we stroll past bottles that smell like shampoo. What did I do to deserve this?

I have to get back to the treat row. And then convince Hattie that I need one. Or a bunch.

Food Lady puts a bottle of flowery shampoo into the cart. Fetch Man turns the cart and heads back to the front of the Treat Place. Uh-oh. That means they're getting ready to leave.

This is every kind of wrong. I spin around and drag Hattie to the treat row. "This way, Hattie!" I bark. "You forgot my treat!"

Hattie lets out a loud sigh.

I jump and pull. "I'll never give up!"

"Fenway, heel!" she commands.

Oh, I know this! I can get what I want by making her happy. I stop jumping and plop onto my bum. I

gaze up at my short human. I tilt my head in that cute way she likes.

"Aw, Fenway," she sings. I can tell from her eyes that it's working. She pats my head, and I give her hand a sweet little lick.

Hooray! Hattie reaches for a delicious-smelling bone. Wowee, a bone is an even better prize than I was hoping for! I can't wait to sink my teeth into it!

We rush back to Fetch Man and Food Lady with the bone. "Please?" Hattie asks them.

Food Lady raises an eyebrow. Fetch Man shrugs. Whoopee! That means they're going to say yes!

I drop onto my bum again. I look up at Hattie, ready to snatch that wonderful bone from her hand. I knew if I tried hard enough, this would work!

But when Food Lady says, "Okay," Hattie plunks the bone

into the cart along with the rest of the stuff.

Wait a minute! She was supposed to give it to me.

This isn't fair! That bone is so close. I can smell it. I can see it. But I can't have it.

This is the worst day ever!

When we get back to the car, Fetch Man puts everything in the trunk—including the bone. On the way home, I make a decision. I'm going to get that bone, and when I do, nobody will ever take it away.

3

THE LADIES

At home, Fetch Man and Food Lady take the bags out of the car. As soon as Hattie unclips my leash, I trot after Food Lady.

She has the crinkly bag with the bone inside. And it's mine, all mine!

When we get to the Eating Place, Food Lady sets the bag on the counter. My tongue drools. My tail goes nuts.

Hattie goes to the counter, too. I hear the bag crinkle. Instead of jumping and whining, I sink onto my bum. Waiting is hard. But it pays off!

"Here, Fenway," Hattie says. She tosses the bone right into my mouth—*chomp!* Finally! We rush over to the sliding door, and she lets me outside.

I sprint down the steps into the Dog Park behind our house. It's a grassy space with a giant tree and a wooden fence all around. I can hardly wait to enjoy my bone!

"Is that you, Fenway?" my friend Patches says from the other side of the fence. She is a white dog with dark patches.

"I don't smell him," Goldie says to her. She's a Golden Retriever. "All I smell is a delicious bone."

Patches and Goldie live in the Dog Park next door. I romp over to the fence. I'm so glad the ladies noticed my new bone.

I let the bone fall to the grass and then peer through the slats. "It's me and a bone!" I say. "It was hard work convincing Hattie to get it for me."

The ladies look at each other, then back at me. "I'll bet," Goldie says.

"Good job, Fenway," says Patches.

"You're a dog who never gives up," Goldie adds.

Gee, I could get used to all this praise. "Thanks, ladies," I say.

Goldie stares at the bone. She smacks her chops. "That sure smells yummy," she says.

Patches noses her. "That bone belongs to Fenway," she says. "If you want one, you can convince Angel to get a bone for you." Angel is their short human.

Goldie grumbles something I can't quite hear.

"Anyway, ladies," I say, eyeing the bone on the ground. "I'll be heading off now. You know, to enjoy the bone."

"Of course," I hear Patches say as I snatch the bone. I prance into the middle of the soft, cool grass.

I'm about to plop down for a good, long chew when I'm startled by horrible sounds. They're coming from the giant tree.

CHIPPER-CHATTER-SQUAWK!

Those sounds can only mean one thing—a sneaky squirrel is coming! I turn around, my fur prickling.

The squirrel clatters down the trunk headfirst and springs into the grass. His bushy tail flounces behind him.

I take off like a shot. "It's called a Dog Park for a reason!" I bark. "No squirrels allowed!"

He scampers toward Food Lady's vegetable patch. Ha! I'll race around the other way.

Just as I'm about to head him off, I hear that horrible sound again. But this time it's coming from the middle of the Dog Park.

CHIPPER-CHATTER-SQUAWK!

I spin around, and I can hardly believe my eyes. A bigger squirrel is about to pounce on my bone.

4

SQUIRREL TROUBLE!

I race toward the second squirrel. "That's my bone, Rodent!" I bark. "Get away! Or else!"

He takes his time glancing up. He does not look frightened at all.

But he must see the tough dog coming right at him. He must hear the warning. Is he waiting until the last moment to make a surprise move?

CHIPPER-CHATTER-SQUAWK! sounds behind me.

Uh-oh! The first squirrel is headed this way! I should have known the two of them were in this together.

I run faster. "That bone is mine!" I bark.

The big squirrel waits until I'm about to lunge. Then he suddenly hops up and scampers across the Dog Park.

The chase is on! "You don't belong here!" I bark. I follow

that squirrel
to the wooden
fence behind
the giant tree.

He leaps. He claws. He clatters to the top.

I jump up and paw the fence. "And don't come back!" I bark. I watch until his bushy tail disappears over the other side.

Whew!

I whirl around and begin trotting back through the grass. That's when I see the first squirrel again. Now *he's* hovering over my bone!

Did he think I'd give up? "Leave that . . . alone!" I pant. "It's not . . . yours!"

This squirrel is just as sneaky as the bigger one. He doesn't move.

He sits next to the bone, calm as can be.

But I'm ready for whatever he's got. I race toward him. "I mean business!"

The squirrel stares at me until I'm close enough to pounce. Then he slowly wanders away as if he just decided to leave.

He speeds up as I chase him, then bolts over the fence like the other one. Whew! Time to hurry back to my bone.

I sink into the grass and give it a lick. At last! But I'm not chewing. I'm thinking.

Two squirrels have tried to take

my bone so far. Hmm. Leaving it in the middle of the Dog Park might not be a good idea.

I'll never be able to enjoy my bone if I'm always chasing sneaky squirrels away. If only there was a way to hide it from them . . .

Aha!

I leap up and run in circles. I'll hide my bone so no one can take it! It's the Best Idea Ever! I just have to find the perfect place.

I take the bone over to the bushes along the far-side fence. I sniff the sweet-smelling mulch. I give it a swipe. Wowee! This would be so easy to dig in!

Then two swipes later, my paw snags an acorn. Yikes! That means this is a squirrel's hiding spot. I have to find a better one.

I wander around the Dog Park, searching. How about under the giant tree? No, squirrels scurry up and down the trunk all the time.

There must be a place that no squirrel would ever look. I'm strolling through the grass when I come to the vegetable patch. I notice damp soil around a tall, leafy plant that smells like tomatoes. Whenever I go near this spot, I get shooed away.

That's it! Everybody knows that

Food Lady's vegetable patch is off-limits. It's the perfect spot to hide my bone!

I quickly dig a bone-size hole, drop it in, and cover it up.

5

RAIN

At lunchtime, I'm inside the house pacing near the sliding door. Rain drips down the glass.

Normally, I'd be sitting next to Hattie's chair in the Eating Place. She loves to secretly drop her crusts so I can gobble them up. But I'm not thinking about Hattie's yummy crusts.

I'm thinking about my bone.

Burying it was a good idea. No one can take it from me. Except now that it's buried, *I* don't have it, either. What fun is having a bone if I can't munch on it?

Every time I gaze out into the Dog Park, I see rain, rain, and more rain. I don't see my bone, but luckily, I don't see any sneaky squirrels, either. They'd better not show up the moment I look away.

"Oh, Fenway!" Hattie calls in her sweet voice.

My tail swishes, and I trot into the Eating Place. Wowee! I bet something wonderful is about to happen. Does she have another bone to give me?

Hattie stands at the counter. "Here, boy," she says.

Sniff, sniff. She has a delicious treat in her hand! Whoopee! I knew it was something wonderful!

I sit on my bum. I cock my head and give her my cutest look.

But instead of tossing me the treat, Hattie holds it over my head. She brings her hand down slowly. My mouth is ready!

But she grabs the scruff of my neck. That's not where treats go!

Oh no! Her other hand is coming down from the counter, and it smells like horrible-smelling drops! Ew! She rubs them into my fur.

My tail droops. What a terrible surprise!

"Good boy," she says, letting me go. The treat sails into my mouth.

Munch! Yippee! Is that ever

delicious! "Thanks, Hattie! That was awesome!" I bark. I rush back to the sliding door. "But what I really want is to go outside and get my bone."

Hattie just looks out at the rain and shrugs.

My ears sag. I know what this means. When it rains, Hattie doesn't open the door to the Dog Park. She only takes me out in the front. And on the leash. I'm going to have to wait.

I hate waiting!

I follow Hattie into the Lounging Place. She flops onto the couch with a book.

I'm about to curl up on the rug when I spy my bone! It's under the couch!

Did I forget it was here?

Wowee! I drop to my belly and wiggle in. My jaws open up and—*chomp!* I back out into the room, my tail high and proud.

I give the bone a few more chomps and—*squeeeak-squeeeak-squeeeak*.

What? I drop that bone, and my tail wilts.

My new bone doesn't squeak. And it doesn't taste like a rubbery toy. This is a toy bone.

For the rest of the day, I'm stuck inside. I pace around the house, trying not to think about how much I want that bone. The real one.

I find my old tennis ball upstairs. I tuck it behind Hattie's pillow and play a game. I snuggle in her blankets, pop out, and grab the ball. I do this over and over. But it's not as fun as digging up my bone.

My tail slumps again. There must be something else I can do.

Aha! On the floor, I discover the fuzzy toy that used to be a bear. Now it's only the upper half, with one arm.

I nose it under Hattie's rumpled sweatshirt, then race around the room once, twice, three times. I throw myself onto the sweatshirt. I pull it off the used-to-be bear, ready to chomp!

But at the last second, I stop myself. I don't want to play with toys.

I want my bone.

6

HOLES

It keeps raining all night. But when I wake up in the morning, sunshine is pouring through the window. "Wake up, Hattie!" I bark. "It's time to go out!"

"Oh, Fenway," she mumbles. She does not sound excited. But the good news is that she heads downstairs anyway.

I trot after her. Hooray! Hooray!
I can finally get back into the Dog
Park!

As soon as she slides the door
open, I dash onto the porch. I sniff
the air—ah! No sign
of squirrels,

only wet dirt and grass. Whoopee, it's great to be outside after such a long, long time.

I sprint into the Dog Park, my paws squishing in the wet grass. I haven't gone far when I hear dog tags jingling on the other side of the fence. "Hey there, Fenway," Patches calls. "Why don't you come over for a sniff?"

"Wish I could, ladies," I call. "But I've got to find my bone."

"You lost it?" Goldie asks.

"I didn't lose it," I say. "I hid it from the squirrels."

Goldie and Patches are quiet for a

moment. Then Patches says,
"Are you sure that was
a good idea?"

"Of course," I tell them. The
ladies don't understand squirrels
like I do.

I romp over to the bushes. The mulch beneath them is soaked, and there's a little puddle shaped exactly like a paw print.

Hey! That's probably the spot where I buried the bone! Wowee, I can already taste it!

My paws get busy digging through the mulch and soft mud underneath. That bone is down here, and I'm about to snag it!

I dig with all my might. The hole is getting bigger and deeper. Pretty soon, I'm tired and panting. My tongue is hanging low. My muzzle is full of mud, but I can't slow down. I'm so ready for that bone!

But as I keep digging, I start to worry. What if I can't find it?

I was so careful about hiding my bone. It has to be here.

But it's not. I lift my snout out of the hole and sniff. My fur prickles with an even worse feeling. My ears do, too.

CHIPPER-CHATTER-SQUAWK!

Uh-oh! Those sneaky squirrels are back!

I speed over to the giant tree. "If you took my bone, you're in big trouble, Rodent!" I bark.

The squirrel is halfway down

the trunk, his black eyes staring. I
know that look—he's totally guilty!
I leap up and scrape the bark.

"Give it back!" I growl. "That bone is mine!"

He stays in the same spot, not moving. He is not the least bit scared. *CHIPPER-CHATTER-SQUAWK!*

I bare my teeth, but it makes no difference. That sneaky squirrel won't lead me to the bone. That means it's up to me to find it.

I wander through the wet grass. That bone could be anywhere. I see another little puddle and dig.

And dig
and dig
and dig.

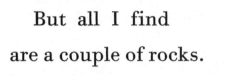

But all I find
are a couple of rocks.

I head over to another
muddy spot in the grass.
I scrape and swipe. I
dig another hole.
But my bone isn't
there, either.

I won't give up, no matter what.
I rush around the Dog Park,
digging in every spot I
can think of. Before
long, the grass is
full of holes. But
I still don't have
my bone.

Clearly, I have to work even harder. Just as I thrust my paws into another muddy spot, I hear the back door slide open. And Hattie yells, "Fenway!"

7

CHASE!

My paws churn up more and more mud. I hear Hattie's footsteps, but I don't turn around. "Not now, Hattie!" I bark. "I'm busy trying to find my bone."

I hear another set of footsteps, too. It smells like our friend Angel.

"Fenway!" Hattie calls again.

"Fenway!" Angel yells.

I sneak a quick peek. They are both running straight at me. They want to play. What rotten timing! "I know you want to have fun," I bark. "But I'm busy. Maybe you can chase me later."

I dig harder. I dig faster. I dig with all my might. This hole is even deeper than the others, and there's no sign of my bone. From the sound of Hattie's footsteps, she is not giving up. She must really want to play. She lunges for me.

Maybe I can take a short break. "Okay. I'll play," I bark. I take off across the Dog Park. "But just for a minute!"

"Here, Fenway!" Hattie shouts.

"Come, Fenway!" Angel cries.

Their voices do not sound like they're having fun. They actually sound angry. What's the matter with them? They got what they wanted. I'm playing the game. Games are supposed to be fun!

I race past the vegetable patch. I weave around clumps of mud. I speed toward the back fence. The game has barely started, and I'm already tired.

As I make a wide arc around the

giant tree, I'm panting for breath.
Hattie and Angel are right on my
tail. I can't let them catch me. I'm
playing to win!

I dive under the bushes and lie
on my belly. I hope Hattie and
Angel won't mind if I take a little
rest.

But Hattie's fingers keep coming
toward me. "Here, boy," she says.

I have a bad feeling about this.

Hattie's face appears. Her dark eyes glare at me. "Bad boy!" she snaps. That's Human for "I'm mad at you!"

Uh-oh.

What's Hattie so mad about? I only wanted to rest. "Okay, okay," I bark, crawling under the next bush, then the next, and the next. "I'll keep playing."

When I get to the farthest bush, I stop to plan my next move. I'll race past the porch!

But right when I shoot out into the Dog Park, Angel's hands grab me. She has me by the collar. "Gotcha!" she cries.

Where did she come from? "Hey, let me go!" I bark.

Hattie sprints over, wagging her finger. "Bad boy," she says again. She scoops me into her arms.

I kick my legs. "Let me go!" I bark. But it's no use. Hattie hugs me tighter and carries me to the house.

8

THE DREAM

I keep barking as Hattie stomps into the Eating Place. She smells mad.

Ignoring my wiggling and twisting and kicking, she plops me into the sink.

When I look up, Angel appears with a bottle of flowery shampoo. Oh no!

"I don't deserve this, Hattie!" I whimper.

I try to squirm away from the rushing water, but it's no use.

Hattie and Angel are both holding me down. The more I thrash, the harder they grip. Pretty soon, I'm soaked and my coat is full of flowery suds!

After a long, long time, Hattie towels me off. When she sets me down, I follow her to the back door. I smell awful, like flowers. But luckily the torture is over, and I can get back to finding my bone.

Hattie wags her finger at me. "Bad boy," she says again. She and Angel head outside and leave me behind in the hallway.

"Wait!" I yelp. "You forgot me!"

I jump and scratch, but Hattie doesn't come back.

How did everything get so messed up? I only wanted to enjoy my bone. Now I can't even try to get it back. Maybe I should give up.

I sink onto the floor with a loud sigh. After all that digging and running and leaping and thrashing, I'm so tired. My eyelids grow heavy, and then I'm dreaming . . .

I'm out in the Dog Park.
Yummy bones are piled
up around the giant tree,

along the bushes, and beside the vegetable patch. They're every- where, and they're just waiting for a hungry dog like me!

Hooray! Hooray! I'm charging toward the nearest bone when I hear—

CHIPPER-CHATTER-SQUAWK!
CHIPPER-CHATTER-SQUAWK!
CHIPPER-CHATTER-SQUAWK!

When I turn around, sneaky squirrels are clattering down the giant tree. Hundreds! Thousands! It's a squirrel attack!

Yikes! Those sneaky squirrels rush into the Dog Park and scatter before I can decide which one to chase first. Some grab the bones piled around the giant tree.

Some snatch the ones along the bushes. And the others head over to the vegetable patch and steal the rest.

And just like that, all those yummy bones are gone.

9

SURPRISE

When my eyes pop open, I'm not in the Dog Park. I'm lying on the floor in the hallway. Was I asleep?

I hop up. I'm in the middle of a wake-up shake when I remember.

My bone is gone. The squirrels took it. And I'm going to get it back. I need that bone!

Food Lady appears. "Oh, Fenway," she says with a frown. Does she feel as bad as I do about the bone? Maybe so, because she goes to the door.

I give her hand a sweet little lick.

Food Lady slides the door open and lets me out. "Now be a good boy," she warns. What's that supposed to mean?

I trot onto the porch and spy Hattie. She's crouched down, patting the dirt.

As I hop down the porch steps, I spy something else.

The Dog Park looks messy and

torn up. The grass is spotted with patches of mud. This must be the work of squirrels!

First they kept me from enjoying my bone. Then they stole it. And next they came into the Dog Park, where they don't belong, and ruined it. Those squirrels are nothing but sneaky. But they're no match for me.

I'm trying to think of a plan when—

CHIPPER-CHATTER-SQUAWK!

A squirrel scurries along the top of the side fence. He dives into the

Dog Park and begins scampering toward Hattie!

I speed over to him. "Leave her alone!" I bark.

When I'm close enough to lunge, the squirrel zigs toward the vegetable patch.

"Oh no you don't!" I bark.

He doesn't listen. That sneaky squirrel dashes under the curly vines. He's headed to the other side, where Hattie is crouched. She has her back to him. She doesn't know he's coming!

"Get up, Hattie!" I bark. "He's coming right for you!" I shoot into

the vegetable patch to
head him off. That
squirrel will not
get my short
human!

I spot him digging near a tall, leafy plant that smells like tomatoes. "I've got you now, Rodent!" I bark.

"Fenway!" Hattie yells. She's clearly upset.

"Don't worry, Hattie!" I bark. "I've got this!"

The squirrel springs up and weaves through the stems. I catch sight of his fluffy tail as he jumps out of the vegetable patch and runs away.

Ha!

I'm romping back through the soil when my back paw hits something hard. *Ouch!* I whip around. Wowee! I can hardly believe what I find.

10

THE BONE

Before supper, my whole family is out in the Dog Park. Food Lady's standing at the smoky-smelling barbecue. Hattie and Fetch Man are sprinkling seeds on the patches of dried mud. We're not going someplace exciting in the car, and that's okay with me.

Normally I'd be playing with

Hattie and Fetch Man, but their game doesn't seem like fun. Besides, tonight I have something better to do. I'm sprawled out on the porch with my bone. And it's even yummier than I thought it would be!

"Looks like you found your bone, Fenway," Patches calls from the other side of the fence.

"What luck," Goldie says.

I trot over. "I did find it," I say to the ladies. "But it wasn't luck. First I had to do all that searching and digging. And then I had to save Hattie from a sneaky squirrel. This bone was a reward for the hard work I did!"

"Amazing," the ladies say at the same time. They sound impressed, even Goldie.

I think about how hard I work every day keeping Hattie safe from squirrels. Good thing I never give up.

"We did some hard work, too," Goldie says.

"You did?" I peer through the slats. Wowee, I see two more yummy-looking bones!

"You gave us the idea, Fenway," Patches says.

"We convinced Angel to get us bones, too," Goldie says. She plops down in the grass and begins gnawing. So does Patches.

Whoopee. Now we can all enjoy our bones!

I'm about to give mine a big chomp when—

CHIPPER-CHATTER-SQUAWK!

My fur prickles. How dare that sneaky squirrel come back!

He's perched on top of the back fence. His poofy tail waves behind him. That squirrel better stay up there!

I grab my bone and race toward him.

"Fenway!" Hattie cries. She rushes after me. She must think I want to play chase.

At the back fence, I let the bone drop and gaze up at him. "Look at me, Rodent!" I bark. "I have my bone back, and you'll never get it again."

As Hattie arrives, the squirrel springs up and leaps into the giant tree. Squirrels may be sneaky, but at least this one has learned he's no match for me.

"Now stay up there where you belong!" I bark. I chomp on the bone.

Hattie scoops me into her arms and carries me back to the porch. What can I say? After all my hard work, my short human wants to give me a break. The barbecue smells amazing, like hot dogs. And I have a feeling it's suppertime.

ABOUT THE AUTHOR

VICTORIA J. COE's books for middle grade readers include the Global Read Aloud, Amazon Teacher's Pick, and One School, One Book favorite *Fenway and Hattie* as well as three Fenway and Hattie sequels. **Make Way for Fenway!** is her first chapter book series. Connect with her online at victoriajcoe.com and on Twitter and Instagram @victoriajcoe.

ABOUT THE ILLUSTRATOR

JOANNE LEW-VRIETHOFF's passion and love for storytelling is shown through her whimsical and heartfelt illustrations in picture and chapter books. Joanne also loves discovering the world with her family by traveling and collecting memories along the way, giving her more inspiration for her illustrations. Her favorite downtime activities are reading YA books recommended by her daughter, looking at TikTok videos of dogs and cats, and watching the Discovery Channel. Currently, Joanne divides her time between Amsterdam and Asia. Connect with her on Instagram @joannelewvriethoff.

LOOK FOR THE NEXT

MAKE WAY FOR FENWAY!

CHAPTER BOOK!

fenway
AND THE
FRISBEE TRICK